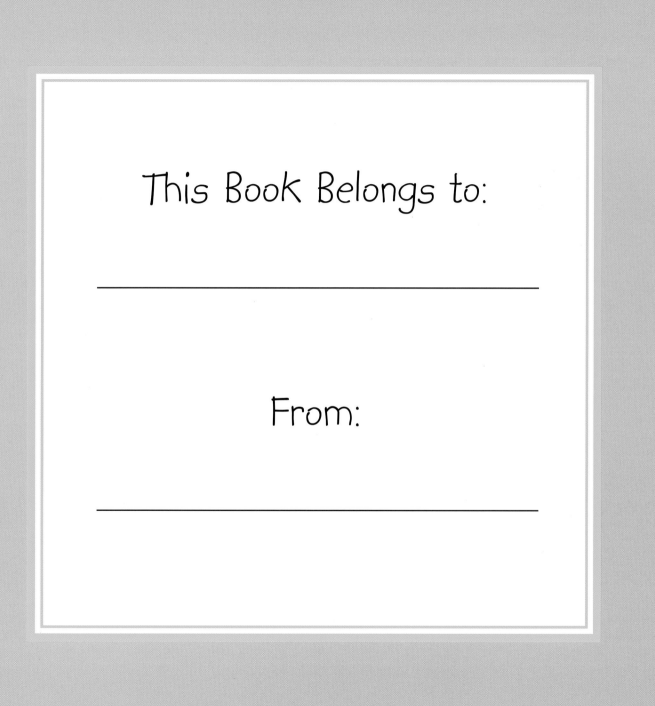

This Book Belongs to:

_____

From:

_____

The Story of Mary

ISBN 0-8249-5546-3

Published by Ideals Children's Books
An imprint of Ideals Publications
A Guideposts Company
535 Metroplex Drive, Suite 250
Nashville, Tennessee 37211
www.idealsbooks.com

Color separations by Precision Color Graphics, Franklin, Wisconsin

Printed and bound in Italy by LEGO

Library of Congress CIP data on file

Designed by Jenny Eber Hancock
Cover design by Georgina Childlow-Rucker

10 9 8 7 6 5 4 3 2 1

The Story of Mary

By Patricia A. Pingry • Illustrated by Stacy Venturi-Pickett

ideals children's books™
Nashville, Tennessee

A long time ago,
a girl named
Mary
lived in the
town of
Nazareth
in Judea.

One day,
an angel named
Gabriel visited Mary.
"You will be the mother
of a very special baby,"
said Gabriel.
"The baby will be
God's Son.
His name will be Jesus."

After the angel left,
Mary ran
to tell her cousin
Elizabeth.
Elizabeth
was also going to
have a baby.

Then Mary
went to tell Joseph
about the baby.
Joseph
would be Jesus'
earthly father.

Months later,
the ruler of Judea said,
"All people must be
counted.
Go to your parents'
birthplace."
Mary and Joseph
had to go to Bethlehem
to be counted.

Mary rode a donkey. Joseph walked. It took many days to reach Bethlehem.

There were many
people in Bethlehem.
There was
no room
for Mary and Joseph.
There was
no bed
for Mary in Bethlehem.

Joseph made a bed
for Mary in a
stable.
That night,
God's Son was born.
Mary called Him
Jesus.

Angels announced the birth of Mary's Son to shepherds. The angels said, "You will find the Babe lying in a manger."

The
shepherds
ran to see
Mary's Baby.
God sent a
star
to mark the place
where Jesus lay.

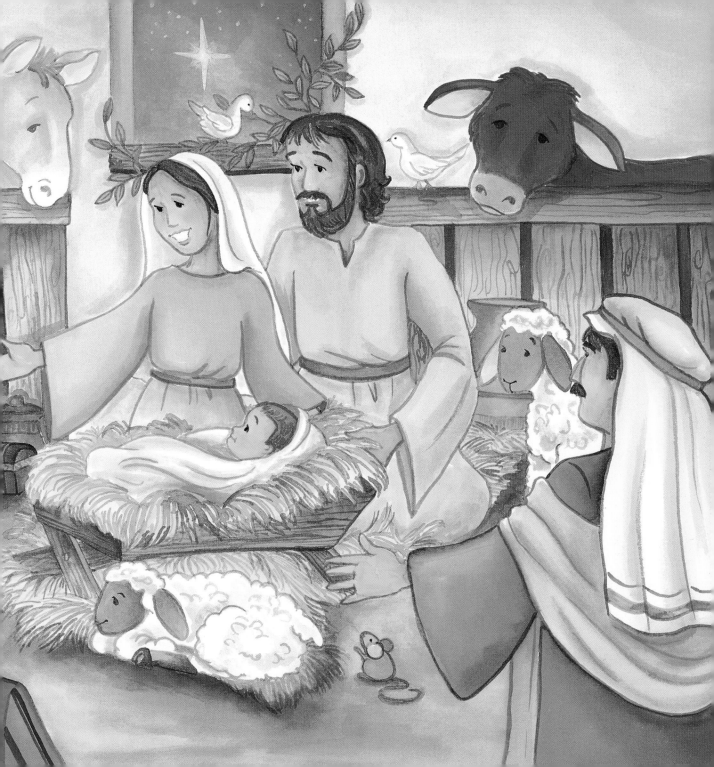

The star led
wise men
to the manger.
They brought
Baby Jesus
gold, frankincense,
and myrrh.

After the visitors left,

Mary held her

baby close.

She knew that

the angel had been right.

Jesus

was very

special.